"Ship of Fools" by Harry J. Bentham

© Harry J. Bentham

2014

twitter.com/hjbentham

Contents

Search Beyond is a compilation

Search Beyond is a series containing science fiction short stories by Harry J. Bentham, started in 2013. While these stories feature recurring characters and settings, they are not episodes in a serialized work or chapters in a book. Each story should be read and reviewed based on its own merits.

Search Beyond stories go through a peer review process to ensure quality. In any book release of *Search Beyond*, at least one story has been reviewed and approved by a number of authors and editors prior to publication and the others have been thoroughly checked to meet the same standard.

"SHIP OF FOOLS" (short fiction)

Only available in *Ship of Fools*

This is taking too long, Sannox thought, throwing data from one hand to the other along the interactive desk in his office as he reclined. *Considering the flash was over an hour ago, we should have left Aldebaran by now.*

His eyes drifted to regard the stars beyond his nearby viewing port. Typically, it would take around half an hour at maximum interstellar speeds to notice even the smallest change in the constellations beyond that port. Specifically, Sannox was awaiting the closing of the gap between two nearby dwarf stars. He continued to check the port, but each glance failed to find his cue for liberation from Aldebaran's gravity.

Everything seems exactly as it had been before! he considered. *The incredible distances at which the constellations stand may render interstellar transit indiscernible to most, but my spacefaring sense is better than that! I know we're not moving!*

Before he could lose patience enough to stand and return to the Bridge in search of the answer, Sannox felt reminded of the competence of his subordinates. *The more confidence I have in them, the more they will have in me in turn,* he thought.

Harmer is, of course, always onto these problems. And Anita is relentless when it comes to chasing challenges such as this. Sometimes, I wonder what they need me for. If there's a problem in the reactor, Harmer needs to reserve the task for himself. I would only complicate things, not to mention burn my hands again, by interfering.

Another minute or so passed, and it was almost an epiphany for the Captain as his impatience returned. His eyes returned to the starry viewing port. *Damn this, I'm contacting the Nest!* He keyed the inquiry into his desk, preferring not to use his voice to interface with the Computer.

"I'm sorry, Captain. The Nest is not available right now," the ship's female persona responded.

Not available? Sannox's disaffection erupted as he stood and departed the office. Through the doors of the War Room and onto the Bridge Deck, the Captain stormed.

"Anita," he addressed his second-in-command, "I thought I ordered us away from Aldebaran."

"You did, sir," she responded, "is there any change in our orders?"

"We have not moved."

"We don't know that for sure. The Engineering Deck reports that the flash sent us to normal interstellar speeds. All systems there are operating normally. The Nest is still down. Considering that we were in combat recently and our reactor array is new, faults are a possibility."

"A Nest fault is serious business in uncharted space, Anita. You should know that. We should come to a full stop and run diagnostics, until our systems are functioning normally. The Nest may be a highly complex dark zone for most of our technical staff, but it is a key navigational instrument and I feel our security is threatened unless it is fully operational."

Anita turned to the aide at her desk. "Initiate full stop," she relayed harshly.

That Technologist, Harmer, better have a good explanation, Sannox thought. "Keep me informed," he reminded Anita, as he turned towards the cargo lift at the ship's spine.

"Sir!" Anita interrupted in bewilderment, and the Captain returned to her.

"What is it?" he demanded.

"I'm just looking into the navigational records," she said, poring over her desk. "They are intact, and they don't tally with what the Engineering Deck has told us."

"Why wasn't this brought to our attention before?"

"There is no policy for this kind of discrepancy. It has never happened before. The navigational records should not have this disconnect with the engine logs. It cannot happen."

Something is certainly wrong here, Sannox thought, feeling a slight tremor already coursing through the deck, travelling up his boots and compelling his legs to a shudder as he steadfastly resisted.

"I'm picking up something big out there," one of the helmsmen reported.

"We're caught in its gravity!" Anita said.

"What?" the Captain demanded.

"The planet off our port stern!"

"Fire all thrusters!" Sannox commanded.

"Already doing that, sir," the helmsman insisted, "it's having no effect."

"Impossible," Anita gasped, "it's a giga-body. It looks and registers as Aldebaran One on the navigational computer, but with nearly a million times the gravity!"

"Flash the star drive!" the Captain enforced.

"Flash sequence started," his helmsman assured.

Of course! Sannox thought, *that solves the mystery. A giga-body would completely anchor us, even with the star drive at work. That's the reason we couldn't move away from Aldebaran as planned!*

"We should keep our speed at maximum," Sannox advised, "we've never encountered anything like a giga-body before."

"I'm not sure any ship has encountered a giga-body of that mass," Anita commented in bewilderment, "I'll study our data on it. We should try to learn everything we can about this blunder, to avoid it happening again."

"Agreed. It's a real mystery. Aldebaran is charted. I would have expected this anomaly to have been discovered and catalogued by now. Maybe it was a dark planet, far enough from its home star to have no signature and only be detected by ships unfortunate enough to get within its gravitational effects. Whatever the case, let's avoid this part of space in future."

Leaving Anita with the haphazard deduction he had created to plug his own confusion at the encounter, Sannox simply left the Bridge through the cargo lift with the aim to seek out Technologist Harmer. When the door to the Bridge had closed, he began to doubt his conclusion. *No*, he thought, *that cannot be right.*

The navigational computer identified the planet as Aldebaran One. Could it have gained mass? Could it have actually grown by – what did she say? Millions of times? It defies physics. Even a star would not be so large. Gravitation doesn't really permit such things to exist. Too much gravity and any object will fall in on itself to form a black hole. Giga-bodies are only a theoretical possibility, supposedly on the brink of becoming black holes. Did we witness a giga-body, or something else?

As he stood on the cargo lift, he changed his mind about where he wanted to go. *Wade is my Science Observer*, he considered, *I ought to talk to him about this. Only he can put me at ease over this.* He keyed in the number of the deck he now considered to be Wade's domain.

The Testing Level was further away from the Bridge than most decks. It was also far less staffed than other parts of the ship, and full of some twenty or thirty eccentrics who had dedicated their lives to the impossible task of comprehending the entire universe. Sannox did not normally go there, with the abundance of predatory alien cadavers and specimens leering over him and making him uneasy. Nevertheless, on this occasion, he felt the only answer could reside there.

Lighting on the deck was pale, ghostly and unfitting for a naval starship's corridors. Greenhouses filled with dangerous plants, animals and things neither plant nor animal nestled behind every transparent bulkhead. *This place is even creepier than the last time I saw it,* Sannox thought. *Biosciences have really given the Level their touch, and it looks like they are testing my tolerance.*

A distant figure emerged, moving impatiently against the unsettling green light beaming from the end of the corridor. He approached Sannox, who stopped. The figure seemed to be examining the floor, as if looking for some lost article. The Captain recognized the mannerisms.

"Wade!" Sannox said, and the figure approached.

"Captain," the man acknowledged, "I wasn't expecting to see you here." Sannox thought the Observer's voice seemed decidedly unhappy. His old friend from the Academy was usually one of the more confident and assuring executives on the ship. To hear depression in Leto Wade's voice was possibly the one thing that could make Sannox feel worse than he already did.

"Wade, I need your help with a problem."

"It's Herb. He's gone!" Wade lamented.

"What do you mean, gone?" Sannox said, forgetting his own inquiry altogether, "he has lost cohesion again?"

"That was my first assumption," Wade said, "but I cannot find any trace of him. His shape-shifting, mimetic nature means he could be any one of us. How do I know you're really George?"

"Listen, Wade," the Captain said, "don't be absurd. I just came here from the Bridge. I need your help with a problem. As our Science Observer, you are as well-trained in astronomy as you are in the biosciences. You are the only expert we have. We just encountered a bizarre anomaly, unlike anything I've encountered before. For all intents and purposes, we ran into Aldebaran One, and yet the navigational computer told us its gravity was millions of times stronger than Aldebaran One."

"This could be connected with Herb's disappearance," Wade began to speculate.

"Connected how?"

"Think about it," Wade challenged Sannox, "we flash to full star drive speeds, yet we get nowhere. We come out of the flash, and we find Aldebaran One, a million times larger than it should be. Do you see where I'm going with this?"

"No," the Captain declared.

"It isn't a problem with the universe! It's a problem with the ship. If we have all shrunk, if we are now a millionth the size we used to be –"

"Stop it!" Sannox resisted, "I've heard enough! I'm talking to Harmer. We're going to get our Nest running again, and find out what's really going on in this part of space."

"Listen to me!" Wade screamed, trying to follow the Captain as he stormed back down the corridor in search of the cargo lift.

"This may be an illusion. I think Herb is creating all of this, including us! You're not Captain Sannox!"

What the hell is this lunatic rambling on about? Of course I'm Captain Sannox! The planet must have grown somehow, the Captain continued to believe, *it's the only explanation I can accept!*

When the doors of the lift had opened, and beckoned Sannox back onto the Bridge, he saw Wade's face radiating from the command desk. "Get him off there!" the Captain ordered.

"He's trying to explain–" Anita tried to protect the transmission.

"No, it is we who have been shrunken," the image of Wade insisted, "more accurately, we do not exist. We are nothing but figurines of the real crew, made from Herb's flesh."

"You're delusional," Sannox rebutted, "terminate visual!"

"This isn't really the ship. Look closer. We are inside a conduit. We are part of a severed tissue from Herb's body, lost in some injury during the battle. It is creating the illusion that you are Captain Sannox."

"No," Sannox said, as the deck began shaking again, this time more violently. His boots started to tremble, and he collapsed into his chair.

"It's the planet!" Anita said.

"We've come full circle," the Captain recognized, "we're getting pulled towards the planet. Our course is wrong. It is taking us even further into the planet's gravity!" He was soon scouring every option he could summon on the command desk.

"What are we doing?" Anita inquired.

"I'm sending a distress signal to anyone for assistance."

"Anyone?" Anita asked, perplexed at this sudden reaching out to Earth after Sannox's ostensible determination to keep the ship exiled.

"The signaling array is not responding!"

I recognize the U-shaped sulfur desert on the side of that planet, Sannox thought, as the ship's violent shaking gained intensity. *Aldebaran One. The yellow desert of Aldebaran One. There is no giga-body. We're on a micro-ship. Or what seems like a mimetic copy of the ship. Perhaps it's a copy, or perhaps it's just a piece of debris, home to a fragment of Herb's tissue.*

Yes, I am but a two millimeter fragment of Herb's tissue, suffering from an illusion. Our whole ship and crew are nothing but a casualty of the recent battle in this sector, a drop of Herb's substance, mimicking what he knew as the crew. Even as I continue to try to reboot what I thought to be the signaling array, the planet is sure to finally catch up with this miniature model, and destroy our ship of fools.

"VERMIN" (short fiction)

Only available in *Ship of Fools*

How did life become so good? Sannox thought, reclining in a natural bed formed from the silky plants of the intoxicating world around him. His memories before the forest remained as little more than a blur, but he often woke with the distinct feeling that he could recall faces, shapes, ideas and sensations through his dreams.

Sometimes, I feel certain that I used to do something else before I got here, something strange, he mused once again. *The araknoids say they created and clothed me, but it often doesn't feel like that at all. Whatever the case, I know that whatever came before could not have been as good as this. I feel a true sense of euphoria here. The air is warm, and sweet as honey. Everything is so bright and colorful that I feel a sense of awe at it, going back as far as I can remember. It is as if my eyes weren't meant to see such beauty.*

I'm thirsty, but I don't care, he realized. *Never mind. What's her name, Ayana, will bring me some of the elixir. She's obviously obligated to look after me, and I have always trusted her without*

any hesitation.

Surely enough, Ayana soon arrived with a crystalline vial. She was a slender figure with voluminous dark hair and pale skin, an ideal female humanoid, just the very fellow traveler that Sannox might have conjured up with the liberty of his thoughts. The vial, which was fashioned in the stylized form of two interlocked fangs, radiated with the sparkling blue revitalizing potion that Sannox craved.

Ayana is fast, Sannox thought, *her race is certainly energetic and strong, and I could think of no-one better to watch over my welfare. Still, I have never been able to count how many fingers there are on her hand, when she does this,* he remembered as his custodian began to administer the vial's contents. *Unbelievable, really, that it takes so little of this stuff to actually quench the worst levels of thirst.*

In an act that Sannox still found strange, however pleasurable, Ayana applied the contents of the vile in her own mouth, then, still holding the potion, arrayed both exceptionally long index fingers at each of her cheeks before creeping towards Sannox's neck. At this point, her index fingers grasped Sannox's neck to hold him steady, and she streamed the sapphire liquid forward onto his collarbone. *Yes, it absorbs through the pores*, Sannox remembered. The feeling of revitalizing freshness coursed through his chest, enriching and energizing him. It was like a fountain of youth, impressing upon him a feeling of immortality.

That really solves my thirst, he thought. With her hands grasping the hanging vines at either side of her, Ayana hoisted herself into the air like a gymnast, ascending into one of the many ornate tree dwellings used by the araknoid people. As she rose, her angelic form almost seemed to radiate a golden color on all her surroundings, leaving Sannox feeling more assured than a newborn in the arms of his mother.

Such a handsome species, and with such grace, Sannox surmised. *If only I, whatever I am, could be more like them. The araknoids are definitely superior beings. They are far beyond us, whatever we are. And they are attuned to nature. Beings so graceful and responsible to their environment must be, no doubt, immortal and enduring.*

As he gazed into the vibrant forest surroundings, Sannox's eyes were drawn to an arch-like funnel of flowering vegetation. *Beautiful*, he continued to think. His wandering sight, at first blissful, suddenly returned in fright to the arch. It had unsettled him somehow. The beating of his heart had hastened, although Sannox did not know why.

Every time he tried to look away from the shadow of the arch, a sensation of unease came upon him, drawing him back to observe it with suspicion. Once, something dark and eerie seemed to advance there, like a procession of spindly fingers waving him on. A malevolent thing seemed to be stirring in the arch, like a shadow among shadows, and Sannox was unable to discern the source of the phantom.

Before he could walk closer to the darkness, in search of the answer, his angelic custodian was descending once more.

"Ayana," Sannox whimpered like a child, "I think I was scared. Yes, definitely scared."

"Do not fear," she said in turn, "the glade will protect you. Do not go beyond it, and you shall be safe. The edge of the glade is guarded by Zozobra. Go beyond the glade, and you shall surely die."

"What's out there?" Sannox asked, still monitoring the eerie shadow among the blue and purple blossoms over his protector's shoulder.

"No more questions," Ayana said, "sleep."

As she caressed his neck, a feeling of immense tiredness began to burden him. A purple, stringy substance had been deposited from her fingertips, and Sannox felt sedated by it. It was almost counteracting the nourishing, energizing effects of the elixir that sustained him. By no will of his own, he was rendered uninterested in the lingering shadows and was being lowered back into the soft bed of leaves by the arms of his sweet custodian.

"Thank you," he almost summoned the will to say, but his vision faded quickly and a strange, bleak dream dawned.

Wade? Leto Wade? Is that you? Sannox thought, when a stumbling figure came into view ahead of him in what seemed like the bluish darkness of the night. In the dream, Sannox was not wearing the natural, soft and silky garments woven by his protector. Instead, he was dressed in a serious utilitarian black jacket and sturdy boots. He had a string of white symbols and patterns on his sleeve and trouser, which seemed every bit as formal as his clean black attire. What they meant, he did not know.

He was squinting to see the face of the stumbling man ahead of him. Now, he heard the man say something. "Captain?" the man croaked from a hideous mask of grey and white strands encrusted in glue or mucus.

Wade, Sannox recognized, overwhelmed by the familiarity of the voice and the face from which it uttered. His friend seemed like some dusty and forgotten statue, and Sannox was drawn with great concern to the pinkish sore at his collar. As he struggled to focus on Wade's neck injury, he perceived two distinct marks. They were swollen, reddish sores on the upper chest and neck.

Sannox recognized the nature of the wounds from somewhere, perhaps a book he had once read, but he could never have anticipated their scale. Fangs had penetrated the flesh of his friend's neck, and something unforgivably foul had been injected. *Some insects do similar things to lay their offspring for gestation in their hosts*, Sannox recalled, *yet it could be something far worse!*

Why did he call me Captain? Sannox thought, in bewilderment at the respect resonating in the voice of the man. *Any reverence towards a creature as simple and as pitiful as me is not deserved*, Sannox concluded. *What am I?*

As he regarded the swelling discolorations at Wade's collar, Sannox's hands wandered to his own neck in fear of a similar fate. When he tried to feel his neck, he instead detected something sharp and hostile striking the back of his hand. Long, bony projections had locked around him like a cage, before two dark prongs came forward once again. The burning of the swellings overtook both hands. They collapsed, numb, and the fangs were now free to ravage his neckline.

Sannox's chest burned with the toxin, and he collapsed. Numb and filled with terror, he was forced to watch the spectacle above. A little lower, he saw an arch-like shape at the entrance to a dark funnel. It was much like the arch of blue flowers, only it was constructed of silvery, slimy threads weaved by the bony hands of shadowy workmen swinging and dancing high above from their many sharp limbs. *Spiders*, Sannox thought, *they're just really big spiders*. Despite the apparent lethality of the creatures, he could think of nothing more than a similarly unpleasant childhood memory of crawling into a long-neglected Wendy house.

"Ayana!" Sannox tried to cry out, overwhelmed by the rush of hostile alien images and concepts as he tried to reconnect with the events of the dream. Any sense of comfort that could have survived through to the dream from the friendly world of the forest was fading for as long as he remained unconscious. A profound sense of discomfort, dread and insecurity at his own nature was growing in his chest.

"Captain," a voice whispered. Searching for its source, Sannox discovered none other than Ayana herself.

"What did you call me?"

"Captain? Are you alright? It's me. Do you understand me? I'm trying to communicate. Is it working?"

"I'm scared," Sannox spluttered. His eyes began to comprehend the surroundings again, and he turned to watch the arch of flowers.

He tried to relax, but Ayana descended on him with an agonizingly powerful slap. "Snap out of it!" she demanded.

"I'm scared," he said, trying to monitor the arch of blue blossoms in the golden sun. Something dark and menacing proceeded there again, and his instincts commanded him to shiver violently, rustling the leaves and thus sending a tremor up the ropes to the suspended dwellings of the araknoids.

"Take this," Ayana said, revealing a vial of some clear substance.

Unlike the blue vial, Sannox did not feel comforted by the clear one. Rather, it made him recede in fear. "Keep it away," he whimpered.

"Come here!" Ayana demanded fiercely, lunging forward with her index fingers outstretched and administering the vial to her own mouth.

Sannox rustled violently in leaves, as Ayana held him steady. With her fingers jabbing Sannox's collar painfully, she streamed the substance onto his chest once more from her own mouth. The same burning sensation from the dream invaded Sannox's veins. It weakened him. Once more, he was reduced to a pitiful, defeated posture on the leaves.

Now, as he tried to make sense of things, he continued to stare at the figure of Ayana. She said something.

"Pretend! Do not let them see!" Sannox believed she had said.

Was that my imagination? he thought, *what is real here, and what is not?*

Staring at the face of Ayana, Sannox watched her eyes turn blank as her very head fell from the shoulders, globs of black blood raining towards him and spewing onto his bed of leaves. Bewildered at the sudden and unbelievable violence before him, he tried to turn his head to identify the one responsible. Wielding a sickle, a second womanly figure was standing. Her face carried the very same likeness as Ayana herself.

No! I don't believe this! Sannox thought, *this is a hallucination! It's all a lie! What is happening to me!* With utterly no feeling betrayed in her countenance, the second figure of Ayana stepped over the butchered body of the first in cold blood, taking hold of the ropes connected to her dwelling high above. Turning his head to monitor her ascent, Sannox saw the majesty of her angelic shape steadily fade, and the golden rope was supplanted by slimy threads attached to the bony limbs of her true form. The hideous workman that had been Ayana continued on its ascent through the trees, unaware of Sannox's petrified stare, and disappeared into a hole woven from its own encrusted silk in a white canopy connecting the dark treetops.

Sannox turned to his own body. He was enveloped, cocooned in the workman's silk, incapable of movement. The floor seemed to be littered with the dried carcasses and skeletal remains of what seemed like small rodents. Like him, other faces protruded from the encrusted silk of the floor and the silver walls. Some had the countenances of emaciated humans, while all the others more closely resembled the whiskered faces of hapless chinchillas and guinea pigs.

How did I leave the glade? Sannox thought in disbelief, *what is this place? Ayana! Let me out!* He tried to squirm free of the cocoon, like a worm, but his body felt immobilized. He saw the arch at the great funnel in the silk, and he knew that he had not moved from the glade at all. The stirring shadow within was exposed, some titan standing tall upon the bony stilts of eight legs, his grotesquely overgrown fangs raised high in the manner of horns and his many eyes bearing an eerie, yellowish luminescence.

The immensely mature spider with long drooping legs much over ten meters, suspended at the arch, was the gloomiest thing that Sannox could ever have imagined to be present. *Zozobra*, he thought, remembering the name given to the dark entity by Ayana. *Zozobra is the guardian, the ruler, the one who will kill me if I try to leave.* It was a limp giant, suspended by the silk of other spiders. Indeed, it seemed as if it would have collapsed on the weak stilts of its legs, were it not for the others who served as aids and beasts of burden to prop its immense body up and serve its every need.

Wait! Sannox remembered, *what happened to the first Ayana?* Hesitantly, he turned to look upon the ground where he thought the first servant had been felled by the araknoid's sickle, at least during his delirium. There, he saw a resting body, dressed in the same black attire that he had witnessed in his dream, and with white inscriptions on the arm and trouser. The face was familiar, but it was not the face of the man from his dream.

"Captain?" the black-clad man said, as he recognized Sannox turning to face him, "do you know who I am?"

"You are–" Sannox began. But his memory had remained blocked, his vision still hopelessly distorted and plagued as the illusion tried to restore itself.

"I'll get you free," the man said, "stay very still."

"I can't move," Sannox assured.

When the black-uniformed stranger had affixed an odd-looking mechanical brace to his knuckles, he aimed his fist towards Sannox's encased body. A glow emanated from the brace, to Sannox's amazement, and the envelope of silk weakened and receded as rays of heat penetrated closer to his restricted body.

"How is that?" his rescuer asked.

"I'm really weak. I'll need help," Sannox begged. As he struggled to stand, he looked up to the malevolent long-legged entity still dangling and stirring at the arch. "How do we get past that thing?"

"Lie back down," was the prompt answer.

Sannox obeyed, taking great care not to disturb the networks of silk spread across the floor of the dark forest. The man, or whatever it was, placed its hands on Sannox's chest as if to attempt to resuscitate him. *His fingers are growing!* Sannox thought, *this must still be part of the illusion! I don't believe it!*

Before he could roll over to escape this apparition masquerading as a friendly rescuer, he was blindfolded by what felt like the silk restoring itself over his face. It strongly pressured him into a fetal position, and the ensuing feeling was of being suspended and dragged gently along the ground.

Although his eyes were covered, he could still see menacing shapes through the white veil encasing him. The one thing he could think about now was the particularly horrible dark shape approaching at his right, as he was dragged in the case. Even as he still struggled to separate dream from reality throughout his escape, he was certain of something evil penetrating the veil of his strange carriage.

For a brief moment, the man-thing dragging him lost control of this carriage of silk, directly beneath the dark shapes of the legs and the eerie pod of darkness upheld by them. Through a slight tear that had developed in the veil, he saw a thick, spiny hair protruding from one of the immense drooping legs of the monster. *Zozobra*, he thought again, *the guardian creature.*

SEARCH BEYOND

When the name of the araknoid ruler passed through Sannox's mind as he lay beneath it, he lost all courage. He was shaking, almost deafened by a strange breathing that descended from the shape above him. *That is more than just a strange, oversized spider*, he concluded. *I can feel the malevolence, almost at an intuitive level. It is as strong as the good I could feel in Ayana, but it is evil, absolutely evil! For a thousand years, it has been this world's very worst embodiment of wretchedness, corruption, malice and greed without parallel. I will never escape its revenge, if I should go beyond its gate.*

Even as Sannox was gripped by the frantic dilemma of whether to fight free from the sack and return to his wretched prison in the silk, the weird sledge proceeded on. Although he could not be sure, Sannox managed to discern a flash of sharp, spidery limbs clawing forward to pull his fibrous carriage on.

So my own rescuer was an araknoid! Sannox speculated. *Perhaps there is a game of intrigue afoot among these spiders. Perhaps I am being stolen from one araknoid ranch to be made the property of another! But then how did my rescuer survive being killed by the other, if indeed some sort of killing took place and was not entirely a hallucination?*

The dragging turned uphill, and Sannox began to feel wet with dew seeping through his carriage of silk. He began to be buffeted from side to side by rocks, and started to cry out. "Stop! Stop! I'm alright here! Whatever you are! If we're out of the den, we might as well stop!"

He's ignoring me! Sannox thought. A minute or so later, the sack stopped, and receded entirely. Sannox would have been stark naked, were it not for the still-encrusted remains of the spider silk covering his body and making him feel still captive to the araknoids. He tried to find the beast that had dragged him, but it was nowhere within sight. Instead, he only found the black-uniformed man who had announced himself as his rescuer in the araknoid den.

He resisted shivering in the cold as he surveyed his surroundings. With the araknoid den left kilometers behind, he was now instead stranded on the shoulder of some rocky grey hill resting beneath a dark and menacing sky. Indeed, the sky appeared to be gathering the wills for a clap of thunder, and its darkness added to the overall inhospitable landscape that Sannox now had to accept as the only reality available.

I want some answers, Sannox decided. "Who are you?" he asked the man in black.

"Captain, I know this is difficult."

"Quit with the fiction! I know this isn't real!"

"You're right," the man said, stepping towards Sannox with a friendly, outstretched hand. "My form is a disguise. It isn't an illusion, mind you, but it is a disguise. Feel my hand."

Taking the hand of the apparition, Sannox accepted that, at least within the events of this conversation, his friend did seem to be what he had admitted. There was no pulse in his hand, and the temperature was much too low to be human flesh, but his friend's hand was indeed one of the most solid and believable things that Sannox had been able to touch lately.

"What are you?" he asked, "you aren't one of them? You aren't an araknoid?"

"No. But I'm not human either, and gladly so, or my situation would have been as pitiful as yours. I'm a member of your crew. I follow your orders. My species is irrelevant. All you need to know is that I am able to change shape at will, and I am never truly what I appear to be."

"Well, at least you're honest," Sannox said. "You call me Captain? Captain of what?"

The man in black hesitated, as if unable to find the right words to answer Sannox's question. "Perhaps we should get a better view?" he finally said. In the ensuing minute of climbing, over the crest of the hill, distant mechanical pylons and towers tall enough to poke holes in the clouds became gradually visible. When Sannox hesitated, bewildered at the sight, the man in black prompted him to continue.

Crowning the dormant volcano ahead, the boot-shaped wreck of the strange mechanical titan stood out. It evoked such a confusing sense of affection or nostalgia that Sannox could find no parallel. *Vast modules at least ten stories in height*, he recalled, *those masts and towers, so majestic. And those two wings filled with docking bays at either side of that – Bridge!*

Anchoring the shipwreck to the volcano, from every direction, a forest of the araknoid silk had been erected, as if to enchain the vessel in the planet's gloom and hold her hostage forever. *I know this ship*, Sannox thought.

Without alerting his crewman, the Captain began to walk towards the ship he knew to be his own. He moved clumsily at first, almost stumbling under the continued effects of the araknoid toxins. The man in black came to his aid, pulling him back on his feet whenever he was in danger of slipping on the rock. Finally, he waved away his crewman's assistance, and walked ahead in determination to be reunited with his ship.

"The port wing has an exposed access bay for you to use," Sannox's alien aide observed.

Now, the alien saw fit to ask, "do you remember who I am, sir?"

Sannox paused, struggling to reconstruct the precise words. *Still foggy*, he thought. "Mr. Herb, of course," he stammered. "Look at this slime all over my ship."

"Sir, it's my duty to point out that we should still be trying to negotiate with the araknoids."

"Negotiate? I think I'll need you to help with that, Mr. Herb. I don't understand their language."

"Thank you, sir."

The walk along the crest of the hill, adjoined to the slope of the volcano itself, took little over forty minutes for both of the seasoned explorers to walk. After this, they came under the shadow of the vast port wing of the vessel. Sannox recognized a distant black dot darting back and forth to convey white fibers along the hull of the ship. *An araknoid workman?* he wondered. He began to see areas of bulkhead entirely repaired by solid formations of silk. *That's some skilled handiwork,* he thought, reversing his earlier judgment that the araknoids had done little more than shovel slime.

"That stuff may be a thousand times stronger than steel," the Captain remembered.

"It certainly is."

"Then their services might be necessary. I think they may have done an excellent job patching some of the lower decks. It looks sealed up pretty good."

"Sir, don't forget about the crew."

Sannox looked at Herb, a look of outrage coming across him as he steadily regained his spirit, "what about our crew?"

"Most of them are still out there."

"Then that's what we'll bargain for. Try to make contact with their ruler."

"Zozobra the Guardian?"

"Yes."

Herb looked uneasily ahead, and from the shadow beneath the gigantic wing some shadow seemed to stir. "Sir, your safety is our immediate concern. I rescued you on Doctor Grady's orders. She is still holed up in the Medical Deck, looking for a solution. I think you should try to get to the west bay, now."

"What's the urgency?"

"Zozobra," Herb said, looking directly ahead into the shadows. "I'll try to delay him."

"No," Sannox said, "if this is our chance to negotiate, it's my duty to my crew to be here, to speak through you to the araknoids and bargain for my crew."

"You would not survive if Zozobra is offended, even slightly."

"Protocol still requires the Captain to make diplomatic contact with any new life forms."

"I insist that you flee, Captain."

A clicking sound emanated from high above, and the limp black legs of the immense, ancient spider began to emerge from the white mists of the silk in the shadow of the wing. The clicking had originated from the creature's raised fangs high above, which now appeared as horns at the crown of a dark pod atop the drooping legs of the degenerated monstrosity.

"Zozobra is talking to you," Herb said, "he's calling you vermin. He is admonishing you. How dare you violate the most sacred place, he says."

"Tell him I understand the technology in the ship. Tell him I can help him use it, if he will negotiate."

Herb began exchanging similar clicks with the enraged ruler, and nodded to the Captain to confirm that his message had been delivered. The araknoid chorus continued to click, and a grave look came upon Herb's face.

"I'm going to have to fight Zozobra," he said, "please run, now."

Weakly, the menace tried to lunge forward over Sannox and descend onto him, one fang aimed fiercely downwards. The attack prompted Herb to drain the last burn from his laser cutter brace against the chitin armor of the beast and push Sannox clear of Zozobra's descent. Instead of impaling Sannox with its downward-projected fang, the araknoid ruler fell against dust and the strands of silk violently.

In the minutes while Zozobra's workmen struggled to hoist high and erect his heavy body again, Sannox was sprinting in the rough direction indicated by Herb. Although his bare feet clapped and ached on the hard stones, he had soon closed his distance to the exposed hull of his downed ship, but could find no entrance as described by Herb.

Damn, this thing is so massive! he thought, as he ran alongside the vast hull in search of any way of boarding the exposed underbelly. *There must be a port! An airlock!* he hoped. *There! I don't know what it is, but I see something like a hatch!* As he raised himself up to reach it, he came to understand that the small square opening led to a maintenance crawlway. He wondered if it was connected to the ship's pressure regulating system, and as such would allow him to enter the innards of the mighty vessel. Before he could decide, he heard the approaching sound of scuttling and clicking. By now, the army of scouring predators behind had to have regained its judgment and chosen to pursue.

Sparing no thought for the approaching shadows surely close at his back, Sannox promptly continued and closed the access hatch behind him. With this, he felt a sense of guilt course through him as he abandoned Mr. Herb to his continued duel with the araknoid ruler. *Now, what is this place like inside?* he struggled to remember as he crouched in total darkness, still too restricted by the limited height of the crawlway to stand as he so eagerly preferred

Wherever he was, it was hardly a reassuring place. There was nothing familiar about it. The silk clinging to his skin and concealing his modesty was weakening, and the thought of wandering the cold metal ship naked made him shudder. His memory of the vessel remained foggy. The shape of it had stirred an acute knowledge of his responsibilities to the immense ship, but the story of its accident on the planet still eluded him. This mystery gnawed at him, and he crawled on like a rat, finding no reassurance in the darkness of the cold metal panels.

Some thirty minutes on, Sannox was accompanied by two flashing lines of orange light at either side of him, faintly illuminating the crawlway as he went along. He also noticed a strange rhythm in the air, much like heavy breathing. At first, it came close to disturbing him, but he soon relaxed with the conclusion that it had to be a mechanical process. *Maybe it's the ship trying to re-pressurize*, he thought. For a moment, he thought a shadow had scampered ahead of him. He reached a junction that had given rise to this sighting, but found nothing unusual. *Was that another human?* he hoped. *Or are those things already inside the ship?*

This latter possibility did not frighten him, but it did greatly anger and then sadden him. It made him feel weak. A sense of embarrassment was engulfing him as he faced the true nakedness of his situation. He had not merely been deprived of clothes. He had been taken away from his station – his sacred duty to his crew. Above all, he had been stripped of his home – this ship. Although its cold metal still seemed alien and uncomforting, some voice within him cried out that it once represented everything he had held dear.

Will this ship fly again? Sannox wondered, depressed as he reconsidered the sight of the vessel on the volcano where it had come to rest. He did not understand how it had been able to fly, or what its purpose among the stars might once have been. The question had never yet occurred to him, with the threat of the araknoids and the fate of his crew his foremost concerns. *I will know everything soon*, he reassured himself. *I will not be at the mercy of this poisonous world!*

Upon finding a translucent molt complete with eight spindly, sharp articulated legs among the machinery where he emerged from the duct, Sannox tried to kick it clear. His exposed toe burned with pain, as he failed to move the filthy shell. *This leaves no doubt that the araknoids boarded the ship. Worse, they may have their own designs on the ship's fate*, he considered. Already, he was connecting their elusive, spidery plans with Zozobra's strange proclamation that the ship represented a holy structure.

Disturbing sounds echoed, as though something was trying to tiptoe unnoticed on the deck above, bumping into containers with its many legs along the way. Succeeding this, there was the loud noise of a klaxon. A loud, sizzling pulse and an inhuman shriek followed. The sound of the pulse had seemed familiar and urgent. Sannox did not know what to anticipate from it, although he surmised that he had heard an araknoid intruder falling prey to the disorder on the ship.

Although he turned every few seconds, in fear of some deadly stalker at his back, Sannox soon reached a door covered by a grid of wires. Behind this daunting barrier, there was a wide, towering shaft of metal with service ladders at each side. Already, the glints of the metal panels were starting to conjure undeserved feelings of security for Sannox. More than this, he felt certain that the lift could take him wherever he wanted to go.

As if his hand itself was already stirred by a memory his mind had not yet confirmed, he dialed a sequence into the touch-sensitive panel at his side. The numbers were promptly accepted there, even though the Captain could not yet remember where or when he had first seen them. Some minutes later, a heavy metal panel descended to meet him. The grid pulled upwards and out of sight, inviting Sannox onto the panel.

The main cargo lift! Sannox remembered in a sudden jolt. *I used to ride the main cargo lift to get around the essential areas of the ship. This place was called the spine, the area where all the most important systems are concentrated – everything from the Bridge to the Engineering Deck. How could I have forgotten?*

Again, he confidently stepped forward and dialed his destination into the panel. *Medical Deck.* As the lift began to accelerate on its way to his target, Sannox began to pass through dark areas. Throughout the entire ascent, he had the strangest sensation of spiders falling from the black void high above his head, and felt certain that the possibility was real. Strange sounds of banging and other commotions reverberated down the lift shaft, as well as yet more pulses and shrieks as araknoids stumbled into the security machinery of the ship.

When Sannox had exited the lift, he was met with flickering lights and the fluctuating hum of damaged power cables. The glowing signs, nevertheless, guided him successfully deeper into the Medical Deck. A source of particular alarm to the confused Captain was a dual-gun security turret. Repeatedly, it would pop out of its ceiling hatch, direct a blue targeting laser beam down the dusty corridor in his direction, and then withdraw back into its hatch. There was a sound accompanying it, an irritating buzzing as it tried to send an instruction to the person it thought it had seen.

Although the malfunctioning turret deterred Sannox for a minute or less as he peered down the corridor, he quickly surmised that it was caught in a feedback loop and would present no threat. For an instant, he thought the laser on the turret had flashed orange and locked onto him, but it quickly succumbed to the fault and withdrew without presenting any further threat. The ease with which he had entered this vital area, leading beyond rows of intensive care stations and into the main office, managed to arouse Sannox's discomfort even though he recognized it to be his only chance of reaching the doctor alive.

Before he could begin to call for the Doctor's help, a dark shape lunged over the desk and set upon him. As eight bony legs locked around him, he struggled to throw himself against the wall in the hope of stunning the unwelcome thing. It was too difficult, as the araknoid warrior continued to pressure him out of the office door and down against one of the treatment beds.

Sannox's arms were hopelessly unable to shield his neck from the ravager, as he was brutally pinned down at the wrists by two of the immensely strong slender limbs of the bristling alien. Now, its venomous sabers entered his flesh, and his neck swelled once more with poison.

As he collapsed on the bed, his vision became a hopeless blur, until the eyes of a dedicated woman steadily began to come into Sannox's sight. His mind was still adrift, unable to find focus on anything in the room, until everything fell dark and silent. He sat up, listening with great care to find any threat nearby.

I'm still in the Medical Deck, he thought, *that's good! And these clean clothes look like my uniform! The Doctor must have dressed me while I was unconscious. But I was injected by that poison again! I must trust nothing I see!*

"Good, you are awake," the voice of a woman arrived from behind. For Sannox, there was no denying the memory of that charming sound in her voice, the sharp look in her eyes or the discipline of her perfectly clipped-back hair. Still, he could not believe in her.

"You aren't real," Sannox said, "you are an araknoid. What do you want?"

"Okay," the woman said, "I'm Doctor Helen Grady. Medical Officer aboard the starship *Traction*."

"How did this happen? What has happened to us?"

"You were injected with an enzyme two months ago. As well as digesting your innards over a period of three months, it is also an effective stasis agent, conserving your nutrients and fluids. If you're wondering why your beard didn't grow, that's the reason. As you must have discovered, it's also a hallucinogen, forcing mammalian species to see exactly what the araknoids want them to see."

"No," Sannox implored, "I know this. What I mean to ask is, what happened to us? How did we get shipwrecked here?"

"A long and tragic story," Helen began.

"Please," Sannox begged.

"Over sixty days ago, we started to suffer serious navigational failures. The ship could not handle the pressures of our unique situation, and started to reject our commands as dysfunctional and false. But that wasn't the problem. The problem was a Nest failure. Upon grazing an unknown supermassive black hole, we were plunged into the interstellar gas clouds gathering at the event horizon.

"The ship's outer hull was seriously contorted and changed by this contact, and several key systems went offline, including half the thrusters. We diverted to emergency landings on three different planets, each more inhospitable than the next. On the third planet – this planet – we had no choice but to open the ship's ducts to re-pressurize the ship. When this happened, the alien entities on the surface must have penetrated our defenses.

"Pretty soon, people started hallucinating as an enzyme was injected into them, rendering them slaves of the araknoids and conserving them as food even without their knowledge or consent. We started to fire on each other, believing one another were aliens. At least five people were killed in that firefight. With paranoia spreading and people building barricades with anything they could get their hands on, you decided to make a truce with the other side – with the aliens.

"In the final ceasefire, a delegation of executives left the ship to make peace with the aliens. When the araknoid ruler violated the truce, all who were not barricaded in safety were seized and cocooned in nests. With Harmer and Mukherjee gone from the Bridge, all authority fell to the Computer.

"Unfortunately, things started to get even worse. Because of the enzyme in the crew's bodies, the Computer's bio-scanners failed to distinguish between aliens and the humans. It quickly started tracking our own crew as threats. Most of the crew are either hostages to the araknoids, or they have barricaded themselves against the automated defenses on the ship. I do not know how many are dead."

Sannox's fist clenched, in outrage. All that Helen had said was true, and the memory of it had been newly imposed on him as clear as day by her vivid account.

"Good," Helen said, "you remember."

"When I get my hands on that swollen parasite, Zozobra!"

"Zozobra?" Helen asked.

"That's what they call the araknoid ruler. Haven't you been in contact with Mr. Herb?"

"No. The net has been down since the Computer took control. That's why you were brought here, Captain. Only you can retake control of the Computer, and release the lockdown on the crew.

The minority of our crew who weren't abducted have been holed up in their hiding places for two months now. If they are alive, I can't guarantee they are sane. You'll have to tell them to come here, as soon as possible."

"I'll get to the nearest Computer linkup station, right away."

"Normally, I'd recommend you stay here to recuperate. But since we're the only two staff available, I have to agree that you try it. Please be careful, Captain," Helen warned.

"I am confident I can handle it, now that this poison is out of my system. Our first priority is control, and next the rescue of every human soul on this planet. Only when we've achieved these two goals, may we think about blastoff. I want you to use every means you have to plan and prepare for the rescue and recovery of our crew. I need that enzyme out of their systems fast, just as you got it out of mine."

"Yes, Captain. I've been working on an aerosol version of the solution, but the question of how to administer it is still a hurdle."

"One problem at a time," Sannox concluded as Helen slid a charged laser cutter into the case on his trouser.

The nearest linkup station is on the other side of the Medical Deck, Sannox remembered, departing the intensive care ward through a barely functioning door. *Hopefully, the Computer is going to be happy to see me. If I am interpreting my restored memory properly, this isn't the first time the Computer has gone berserk.*

Unfortunately, the main green-glazed door providing access to the linkup station was not functioning, but the glazed wall at the side offered no resistance to his hand laser cutter. Attaching the weapon's cuff to his knuckles, he pressured it and quickly melted a circular point to access the station. For a moment, he waited for the globs of molten glass to cool, and then stepped across to dial his codes into the station panel.

Good! Sannox thought as he keyed his commands into the system, *you recognize me! Now, release the crew from their lockdown and switch security to perimeter mode. Initiate auto-repairs and reactivate the internal scanners. Send continuous reports on enemy threats to the Medical Office. Now, time to give word to every soul on the ship with a broadcast.*

"All hands, this is Captain George Sannox," he began through the audio alert system, "the security lockout on quarters has been released. If you are able to proceed, arm yourselves and report to the Medical Deck now. Please remain calm and take care. Some of the crew may be experiencing delirium. Use extreme caution when interacting with others.

"You will all need to pass through a Computer security barrier at the location I am sending to all terminals. Be advised that some systems are not functioning correctly. Watch for the whole spectrum of threats, personal, technological, alien. Trust no-one but the Doctor. Listen to her and do as she tells you. End of broadcast."

Now, he thought, *I have to get the external net back online. I won't attack the araknoids. They still hold my captive crewmen and I won't attack until they are free, but I will try to re-establish contact with my crew. Harmer! I must contact Harmer! That Technology Officer has the answers to our situation.*

Immediately upon authorizing the Computer to restore the net, the inbox was filled with requests. Flashing brightly at the top of the list, Sannox's hand moved on a linkup request signed with

Technologist Jon Harmer's ID code. The ensuing audio buzzed at first, and finally stabilized, although still jumping and fluctuating throughout its duration.

"Traction! Traction, come in!" the voice from the other side called.

"Harmer, where are you?"

"I'm in –"

"Your signal is garbled."

"Sorry, George. How about now?"

"Just get on with your message, Jon."

"Herb and I have secured a truce with the araknoids. I've managed to get star engines two and three back on-line! Controlling this equipment remotely, I've created some nice lighting shows and convinced the Guardian creature that I possess magical abilities. He believes it!"

"No, Harmer! Zozobra and the araknoid government are liars! We cannot trust any truce we make with them. They broke their word once already and we can't make the same mistake again. If we don't gather our crew together within the next thirty days, most of our people could die, no matter what deal we make with the araknoids."

"We have no choice but to make this deal, sir."

"Where are you?"

"We're outside. You should see this, sir. The araknoids are circling the ship in a religious gesture. It is almost as significant as the Islamic Hajj, or something."

Sannox spent some seconds poring over the scans he was able to obtain through the net, whereupon he confirmed that some million araknoid beings had gathered and were indeed moving in a vast circle around the wreck.

"Harmer, what is the status of our engines? How ready are we for blastoff?"

"The ship would need to be sealed and re-pressurized, and fuel nozzle three is a wreck. We can't take off with thrusters. They are too badly damaged. We will need to have our full star engine array operational before we attempt blastoff. Even then, I can't guarantee we will survive, sir."

"Here is what I want from you, Harmer. I need you to convince the araknoids to repair the nozzle with their silk and seal any remaining breaches in the ship. Promise them a miracle in the skies, and tell them they must vacate the ship for the magic to work. Promise Zozobra whatever he asks for in return for these rituals. We don't necessarily have to deliver on all of these promises. I'm preparing an auto-controlled disc operation and readying weapons in case things get bad. Alert me at the first sign of trouble. I'm transferring this uplink to the Medical Office. End transmission."

Out of the linkup station, Sannox returned to Helen Grady, who had only bad news to deliver. "Captain, I may have been overly optimistic," she said. "The enzyme is much less uniform than I thought. We could be seeing deaths from our crew within twelve hours. The araknoids may begin to feed on our captive sailors at that time."

Sannox swallowed in displeasure. *This changes everything,* he thought, his hand contacting the interactive pane of Helen's desk and transferring the linkup screen from the authorization point across the Medical Deck. *I have to notify Harmer. No, he must be busy with this stunt of convincing the araknoids to accept the miracle. There's also no telling how long this disc salvage operation will take. I have to begin now, regardless of the situation*

on the ground!

"Helen, I want our crew back aboard, right now!"

"Sir, no one has arrived at Medical yet, even after you released the Computer lockout on their quarters."

"It doesn't matter. How much of the antigen have you synthesized to fight the alien enzyme?"

"Twenty or thirty liters."

"Should be enough," Sannox said.

"I can't guarantee that," Helen said, "most of this supply was supposed to be redundant, since you did request I synthesize the chemical for delivery in aerosol form."

"How many sites are the crew being held at?"

"Most of the crew is held at the main nest, where you were held. Aside from the main nest, there is a second site constructed from silk on a cliff face, about fifteen kilometers off the main nest," Helen indicated, with the help of the detailed maps radiating from the pane.

"Alright, since it holds most of the captives, we'll load the gas onto the discs and carry out a drone evacuation at the main nest in thirty minutes. We'll raid the secondary nest in an hour. The cliff site is less of a priority, because there are fewer captives there. I suggest we raid it on our way out. That is, as long as Harmer and his araknoid followers are working quickly enough out there to fix star nozzle three in time."

Sannox, unable to countenance simply waiting in the dark for the disc mission, reactivated Harmer's channel to snoop on what was happening outside.

"The sacred nozzle is part of the divine geometry of the sacred palace," Harmer was proclaiming authoritatively. *"Without this artifact restored as we have restored the walls, there can be no redemption."* At his side, the spider form of Herb clicked frantically, stirring the army of crawling workmen to action amidst a forest of silk to reach the damaged nozzle of star engine one. *"The inheritance of Zozobra is imminent! Soon, the sacred geometry will be done, and the ancestors will return for your counsel!"*

The speech went on, and the minutes counted down until Helen approved the start of the operation.

"Discs one to nineteen ready and equipped for launch," she said.

"Let's just hope the bots on the rescue discs are more enticing than whatever the hostages are hallucinating."

"Your voice and the antigen should make an effective team," Helen nodded.

"Launching discs one to nineteen! I'm estimating thirty minutes until phase one is complete."

Again, Sannox's attention turned to the live audio and video feeds represented on the linkup screen. Harmer's voice was continuing to preach. *"Look to the skies. Divine emissaries are coming forward!"*

The sounds and images of the discs moving out reassured Sannox, as the araknoid pilgrims clamored in awe. A heavier clicking interrupted, and its rhythm rang contrary to the crowd. Herb's voice muffled from the cast of his spider body through the feed. Sannox froze with uncertainty, remembering the grave news that Herb had last delivered. *"Mr. Harmer, Zozobra is saying you are a liar and a charlatan. He says these carriages carry vermin. They are being sent for stealing."*

Sannox could no longer just stand by and listen to the audio feed. "Harmer, get out of there!"

"He's right!" Herb's voice interceded, *"I'll cover you!"*

Immediately the clamor turned to a fierce rush of violent clattering and crashing like the roaring approach of a million machetes. A forest of spiders was advancing on Harmer. *I won't lose a single man*, Sannox resolved, pressing the ship's laser transfer beams to life in an improvised defense.

"What are you doing?" Helen asked.

"Improvising. Don't question me!" the Captain roared, turning to the Computer herself as his support. "Computer, don't let those freaks get near your Technology Officer. Shield him with the transfer lasers!"

"Complying," the Computer's voice affirmed.

Searing sounds followed, accompanied by mass shrieking and chattering among the assailing army.

"Computer, is the ship pressurized?"

"Affirmative."

"Is the starboard engine nozzle repaired?"

"Sorry, sir. Unknown material is lining the nozzle."

"Sounds about right. Prepare a cold flash sequence!"

"Sir," Helen interrupted, "we haven't recovered any of the discs yet. We're deviating from the plan."

"I'm aware of the situation, Medical Officer. We can easily recover our crew from the surface once we're in orbit. I'm confident the laser lock on the discs will hold." The Captain's thoughts quickly returned to the fates of Harmer and Herb. "Harmer, come in!"

"Captain! I'm with Herb in one of the pressurization reseals. We'll be with you in half an hour!"

"I know the feeling," Sannox muttered under his breath. *Now, to get this thing into orbit before we go through this whole ordeal again*, he thought. "Computer, what is the probability of a safe blastoff from our current position?"

"Zero percent."

Sannox froze, unable to reconcile this cold response with his present will.

"But," the Computer's female voice continued, *"ventral thrusters are now on-line. If they can get us vertical, we stand an eighty-nine percent chance of successfully achieving orbit."*

"Execute now!" the Captain ordered.

A disturbing tremor coursed through the deck, and Sannox recoiled as he felt the deck angling steadily. At forty-five degrees, he and Helen had grasped the nearest supporting rails on the fixed diagnostic beds for support. Sannox closed his eyes, half anticipating disaster. At ninety degrees, he relaxed with the knowledge that the artificial gravity plating had finally kicked in. The entire vessel now stood vertical atop the volcano. *The flash has begun*, Sannox thought. *We're gaining altitude! Five kilometers! Ten kilometers! Fifty kilometers! A hundred kilometers! Three hundred kilometers! Reminds me of the ancient rockets they used to reach the Moon!*

Upon anchoring herself in orbit, the ship began circling over the region that held her captive crewmen. In a moment of satisfaction without comparison, Sannox sighed with relief at the newly received lists of rescued crewmen, all having crawled aboard the nineteen discs without further disruption. *The stasis gas was enough to keep the araknoids away, and the antigen made them sober like a blindfold being ripped from their eyes. It must have been a marvel of a sight to see the lights of the disc waiting to take them home, even amidst the tangled web of their situation! That's over eighty percent of the entire crew, all in stable condition*, he thought, reclining on one of the beds. *I know it could have been far, far worse.*

"That's okay sir," Helen said. "You should take a break now that the worst of it is over. I've got it from here. I won't stop sending discs until every human on the surface is recovered and brought home to bed," Helen assured. "I'm launching the remaining discs to the cliff site. The total crew evacuation looks successful so far, but I'm detecting dangerous levels of the enzyme still in the systems of our recovered crew. Whole new containers of antigen are being synthesized and filled as we speak."

Even as Helen continued to speak, a feeling of immense tiredness was chasing Sannox until it finally overcame him. His body had been filled with poison for two months before its sudden detoxification. His role in the evacuation was done, and he could be in no better place for recovery.

Hours later, the darkness had subsided and the Captain's eyes were open once again. All that had happened seemed as little more than a dream, and the last clear memory in his mind was of himself witnessing an emergency at the Bridge. *The Bridge*, he thought, wistfully.

His every step seeming to reaffirm his return to the right life he had chosen to lead, Sannox boarded the cargo lift, devoid of any trace of the infestation that had plagued it. With it, he ascended until he found the shining gate, summoning him back to the chair and the radiant command desk that he knew to be his right station.

"THE WIRE" (flash fiction)

Originally reviewed on February-March 2014 in *Quantum Muse*

Into the heavy cargo lift platform, George stepped. His mind was wandering. For a moment, he nearly forgot where he wanted to go. Nevertheless, he had already dialed in the identity of the deck, and the lift was in motion.

No sooner than George remembered his intent to inspect the Storage Deck, the lift was in free fall. Already, it had plummeted twenty decks in less than one second. He had to escape, before it was too late!

George's efforts to halt the lift via the control pad were unsuccessful, but enough to cause the platform to falter and slow. In this window of uncertainty, George was able to reach over the rails of the cargo lift platform and grip hold of the rails at the entrance of a crawlway.

The cargo lift rail under his boot abruptly disappeared. Sounds of screeching metal followed, as the platform plummeted a further twenty decks and ended with a savage crash. This spurred George, now sweating feverishly, to heave his body into the crawlway. Where the crawlway led, George did not know. In a ship of such incredible size, no-one could.

George crawled forward in the confined space of the slim metal passageway. A massive chamber came into view, as mighty and as mysterious as a cathedral interior. His hopes were restored as he imagined determining his location from there.

What lay beyond the entrance to the chamber puzzled George as much as the passageway itself. There, a pole upheld a coil of shining metal. It was wider at the base, narrowing to the point of a gleaming orb at the crown in the design of a Tesla coil. He steadily remembered the nature of such a device, although he had never witnessed one.

Removing the pane from his belt, George activated the radio feature. A blinding flash followed, and he opened his eyes to find himself some meters back from his original position. Astonished, George accepted that he had been shocked by the coil and his pane had slid more than ten meters away.

Ahead of George, a dark shape moved. What had at first seemed like part of the mass of cables and junk in the corner changed position, rearing up in the manner of a cobra. As George moved ahead to investigate, the shape changed again, positioning itself upright and turning to face him.

The monstrous mass of dark cables rose higher and higher, ever clear in its resemblance to a snake. Whatever its origins, the creature's self-determined purpose was announced as it drank bright buzzing discharges of electricity from the orb of the coil.

Losing interest in the coil, the serpent slithered away, returning to the heap of massed "nano-wire" repair supplies in the dark corner of the chamber. Recognizing this self-assembled animal and its fountain of youth as two deadly threats to his escape, George saw no alternative than to pull the plug.

With the coupling at the base of the coil exposed, George went ahead without hesitation. Tugging the buzzing cable free, he instantly heard a rush from the junk at the corner of the chamber. The snake was returning. Without turning to confirm the monstrosity was charging, he began to climb the coil.

George had felt certain that the snake would not strike furiously at its own source of nourishment, through fear of damaging it. But, to his surprise, the amalgam of machines attempted to follow, arcing around the bars of the coil to follow George like a great predatory snake among the branches of a tree.

At last, the hostile thing began to disassemble as it lost power, and weakened on the bar of the coil. Its reaching head, if it could be called a head, split into a number of flailing wires as George continued to climb away.

To conclude the strange encounter with this strange assemblage, this accident born from the infinite jungle of the technium, George leapt down from the coil to reclaim his pane and restore contact with the crew.

"Anita," he said, "Anita, come in. This is the Captain."

"Sir!" she responded, "we'll get to you as quickly as possible."

"NO SOLUTION" (flash fiction)

Only available in *Ship of Fools*

The lost space vessel *Traction*, once a feared warship of Earth, now disgraced and displaced thousands of light-years from home with almost no hope of return, slowed cautiously. Her racing telemetry probe had exploded in a gleaming white streak, sending warning of some enigmatic barrier dead ahead. Finally, she drew to a complete halt before the probe's trail.

Inside the armored Bridge, a pyramid-like fortress at the back of the immense ship, Captain George Sannox rose from his chair at the glowing display panel of the command desk.

"What happened?" George demanded.

Anita, the disciplined second-in-command, rotated her seat to face her Captain. "I believe it's a distortion or instability in the space time continuum," she posited. "We must not trust what we see."

"Why?" George challenged.

Jon, the ship's senior engineer quickly interceded. "A cosmic bubble," he said, "according to theory, literally anything could be inside it."

"Anything?"

"There might be a black hole trapped on the other side," Jon continued. "In such an event, it would crush us instantly if we passed the threshold. There could be a miniature copy of our entire universe, or an enlarged one. Alternatively, it could be a copy of only one part of our universe, or a part of our universe that is in another time frame. It could be anything!"

"How do we go around it?" George requested.

"There is no way to tell how large it is," Jon lectured, seemingly pleased with himself, "it does not register on our sensors, so it would be a nigh impossible task to take any measurement of its diameter. Unless, of course, we take a look inside."

"You saw what happened to our probe," George breathed in disappointment.

"No," Harmer argued, "what we saw was most likely just an illusion, brought about by some temporal or spatial effect when vehicles pass through the threshold. We may have seen some possible fate of the probe in the bubble, but it is by no means certain that this really took place. It is safe to go inside."

"Sir, I strongly object to this idea," Anita growled in George's ear, "it just isn't worth dying for."

"I'll go with you," George bounded, filled with curiosity.

As the two officers rode the cargo lift away from the Bridge, George began to revisit his decision to go on the strange reconnaissance mission. It could mean his death, and thus his abandonment of the precious ship that had become his home. Then again, the mission could also be the only way to ensure the safe passage of the nine-hundred or so officers aboard. Finally, he put his personal reservations aside in favor of his crew's future.

The two men went on to pilot a glittering blue visitation disc, one of the nimble craft typically employed to land or transport effectively back and forth from planets, flying out of the bay doors of the ship and ahead along the blazing trail of the apparently destroyed telemetry probe.

With their immense mother ship getting ever more distant behind them, the disc moved on until it reached the first outer layer of the cosmic barrier. Passing through the threshold turned out to be one of the strangest sensations Jon or George had ever experienced. Instantly, all things had radically altered in hue. It was as if all energy had transformed. Lights adorning the controls that were ordinarily yellow had become blue, and bulkheads that had appeared gold turned silver. Like a clap of thunder, there fell a feeling of intense spatial sickness on both of their heads, resulting in piercing headaches.

Jon reached for the controls, taming the disc to a halt.

"Alright, we should leave now," George gasped, sweat streaming down the reddish hair of his temple.

"Sensors say the bubble is only fifty kilometers in diameter. From inside, anyway," Jon read from his console.

"What do you mean, from the inside?"

"It is possible for an object to be sized differently on the inside, of course."

"Fascinating," George said, massaging his temples. "Now, let's leave."

"I'm getting some strange readings to stern," Jon warned.

"Let's take a look," George announced, rotating the craft to face back towards the threshold where the source of the confusion lay. There, directly ahead, a bright light began to shine, and the glowing silhouette of their own mother ship's structure pierced the black of space. The silhouette of white was replaced by the emerging, gigantic bow of *Traction* as she rode through the barrier.

"Evading!" Jon announced, clutching the controls. The disc dived, narrowly escaping the plunging hull of the gigantic vessel.

The disc adapted to face the immense, moving hull of *Traction* once again, and the three channels of the ship's star drive exhaust fumes fluctuated dramatically. The ship plunged deeper into the spatial disturbance, as if dragged by its incredible weight, and a peculiar glow gripped every expanse of the hull as it did so. Its course twisted until the vessel began to slow, leaning feebly to the side. Finally, the entire ship exploded in a dazzling blare of star drive fuel.

As the weight growing in George's heart compelled him to kneel on the deck in hopelessness, he felt the heat of his lost ship pass through the disc and away into the darkness of forever. Now, he knelt, staring with a mind stunned by confusion and disbelief at this untimely end to the crew he had accompanied on so many adventures. He tried to imagine that it had been a mistake. Perhaps it was another ship! No, it was no comfort. He had to face the reality that this was the end.

"Look!" Jon pointed, bringing the disc back into position to watch a new object come steadily forward, an almost mirror image of their own very disc.

"What is it?" George asked, futilely trying to conceal his angst in the presence of his loyal officer.

"Our disc!" Jon said, plunging George into yet more confusion.

"What! That's impossible!" George cried.

"It's gone!"

Indeed, just as Jon indicated, the disc had glistened and vanished as it touched the barrier, in a bizarre vision of space that George could not understand. Jon, however, was quickly steering the disc back along its original course, passing back through the barrier and returning to normal space.

While George Sannox struggled to understand what he had just witnessed, the shape of *Traction*, intact and fully functional, returned into his sight ahead. He rubbed his eyes, unable to pick an explanation, before Anita's voice returned from her apparent grave to greet him over the disc's audio link.

"Disc One, we saw you explode! What happened?" she said frantically.

"Anita! Take the ship away from the disturbance, immediately!" George commanded.

"I think I understand," Harmer mused, discerning the pattern of the strange occurrences that had been witnessed from within the disc and from the Bridge of *Traction*.

The disc had entered an area of space where the physical constants were different. As Jon's log would later tell, "perhaps there was a temporal difference with that. With time fast within the cosmic bubble, the disc had encountered the accelerated future *Traction* entering and being destroyed by the stresses of the transition. With time slower outside the cosmic bubble, *Traction* had similarly observed a version of the disc accelerating beyond its mechanical limits inside the bubble, thus being destroyed on impact.

"The reality, however, was that the disc passed back into the regular universe, thus reclaiming its own integrity in that universe. Mended by its escape from the cosmic bubble, the disc was able to warn *Traction* and thus reverse *Traction*'s own projected fate within the cosmic bubble."

BONUS STORY: "COMPLIANCE" (short

fiction)

Only available in *Ship of Fools*

George was waiting at his seat, outwardly attempting to appear patient and satisfied, yet inwardly burdened by a growing sense of irritation and confusion at his unexpected situation. By some unknown means, he had found himself not on his dear ship but back in the dreaded custody of the earthbound "Authority".

How he had managed to leave the Bridge of his ship only to take up a seat in the stifling surroundings of this dark office remained unknown to him, but he was determined to find the answer. Perhaps, robbing him of his competence and his memory, *they* had seized him and returned him to Earth for trial. Perhaps, as part of the Orwellian regime *they* had orchestrated in their search for him, all that he had thought to be true was nothing but an illusion, and his true fate awaited him in the unwelcoming confines of this office.

They want me for the mutiny, George surmised in the privacy of his own thoughts. *I know this place. This is the main office of a so-called compliance center, the kind of place where they send the unemployed, deserters and other offenders regarded as potential threats to the Authority.* He looked to a notice panel attached to the wall:

ANY FAILURE TO COMPLY WILL RESULT IN MEMORY ERASURE

Soon, the name "George" was called, and George rose and walked compliantly to satisfy the advisor who had requested him for review.

"Why are you here?" the advisor asked, just as George seated himself at the desk. It puzzled him that neither he nor the advisor had introduced themselves, and yet the interview had already begun.

Sensing a trick question, but still unsure why the man would ask such a silly thing of the Captain of a starship, George gave an equally silly answer. "I'm out of work," he said. *That will do*, he thought. *It's the truth, anyway, as far as I can tell in this supposed predicament.*

"How do you feel?" the advisor asked, with unwelcoming grey-blue eyes staring intently into George's own.

"Bored," George said. *And that's the truth too*, he thought.

The advisor nodded, as if pretending to be absorbing every innermost thought from George's own head. "You don't belong here," the advisor expounded self-importantly, in what seemed like an irritating and unhelpful cliché to George.

This use of exhausted, false and arrogant words was instantly recognizable to George. Words designed to give the appearance of expertise and help, while supplying neither. *He's conceited,* George thought, *he thinks he is some kind of expert, and it has gone to his head. Who does he think he is?*

"What is teamwork?" the advisor asked.

"What?" George responded. He was alarmed to have been asked such an abrupt question that had no connection to the earlier comment.

"What is teamwork?" the question came again.

"Teamwork," George began, "is when people coordinate their actions to achieve a shared goal."

"No," the advisor reacted with frustration, "again, what is teamwork?"

"You'll have to be more specific about the definition you are using," George suggested.

"That came across as condescending. Now, tell me what skills you have," the advisor said.

Is this another trick question? George immediately thought, *and will he resist my answer as some kind of psych test again?*

"For example," the advisor continued, "I'm honest and forthright. My job is to make money."

Then what do you need me for? George thought. *What is this absurd meeting about?*

"I'm doing everything required of me," the advisor said, further confusing George with yet another non sequitur. "I know you think you know best, but you are not allowed to judge," the advisor went on, asininely.

What is this? George thought, now unable to prevent his eyebrow from elevating in disbelief at the advisor's continued sense of proficiency and invulnerability from criticism. *Why is this clown pretending to help me, if his only goal is to praise and help himself?*

"I have arranged an interview that you must reach," the advisor went on, "you will be getting a ship to ALM Prime. They'll have enough use for you. But first, I expect you to plot a course."

At the advisor's touch of a panel on the desk, one imaging pane displayed the face of a third individual. The image was sufficiently degraded that George could perceive little further detail, at present. Whether the person displayed was male or female, or whether they were human or artificial, remained obscured from George's ability to determine.

George tried as carefully as he could bring himself, in his boredom, to listen to whatever this individual was attempting to convey from a whole star system away. The interference in the image and sound was now unmistakable to George. *It is being grazed by a black hole. That is why most of the trans-radio signal has been destroyed in the process*, he understood. *How incompetent could the goons running this office really be?*

"Well?" the advisor said, "take the call."

I'll do my best, George thought. "Hello," he said plainly through the trans-radio link, unsure what this communication was meant to accomplish at all.

A garbled reply emerged back. "Hello George," George thought he heard. "Listen, don't go for this interview. The compliance center is just trying to get you to commit to something that won't be possible. ALM Prime only employs local staff. You could never commute by star-drive each day to this job. Don't tell the advisor."

"I think I can get to the site," George countered, sensing the advisor's fury at his lack of enthusiasm for the flight, "but I'll need to plot a course."

"Plot a course, and get back to us with your answer. If it is economical, we can make the arrangements," the distorted electronic words came through from ALM Prime.

Abruptly, the imager darkened to grey. The audio shrieked, buzzed and finally ceased. "They think I can't get to the site," George said, "and it might not be worth the flight."

"You don't want to work, don't you? You destroyed that opportunity on purpose," the advisor said with an irritated scowl.

"No, I just need to plot a course and get back in contact with them."

"I'm cancelling the interview," the advisor said. "You don't need to contact them. From now on, you will come here every day. You will remain at a search station every day, all hours, until you get back into work."

The advisor indicated a panel on the desk beside George's hand. "Sign here," he said. With a quick scribble of his finger through the interactive panel, George complied.

"I expect you back here in a week," the advisor said.

I suppose I can do nothing other than comply, George thought. As he departed the office, arrows were immediately apparent on the display panels of the walls, directing him to where he was next required to go. *Until I can learn more about this station and determine a means of escape, I am a prisoner here.* As he continued through a corridor, he saw the closest thing to a window that might have existed at this office. Thin slits, through which only the dark depths of infinity stared back at him. *Space, the ultimate prison*, George recalled.

After allowing the arrows to guide him for some thirty minutes in the vast and seemingly empty station, George encountered another stretch of corridor. Here, suspended bodies were arrayed in illuminated blue stasis cylinders along both walls. Among them, a single such tube glowed green, and there George encountered a luminous yellow name:

GEORGE SANNOX, 23, SOLAR NAVY GRADUATE

Graduate? George thought, *have I travelled back in time? No, such things are not possible by any technology. This has to be another trick, orchestrated by the psychs during my incarceration here. Are they trying to drive me mad? Are they really attepting to distort my perception of reality? The advisory appointment was confusing and disorientating enough, without having to be followed by this.*

George stepped into the tube. As the electronic stasis field enclosed around him and touched his skin like cold water, his eyes were shut in artificial sleep – the kind of debilitating sleep that

George had believed to be reserved for only the worst convicts. Even still, a disjointed nightmare began.

It seemed like only a brief flash of images. There was the surface of a planet less than comfortable, immediately within George's view. There were thin red streams of molten rock creeping over blackened crust, and billowing fumes surging towards George's face. In the dream, George was encased in a tube, exactly the same as the stasis cylinder he had just recalled sealing himself inside for sleep. However, in this new place, the adjacent tubes and their contained human bodies were not aligned in rows as in the corridor, but rather formed a circle and were part of a larger circular layout. It was only though a hideous tear in the metal frame of this habitation module that George was able to witness the brutal surface of the planet outside. Just as a sense of suffocation began to overrun him, the electrical field suspending him in the cylinder was gone. He stepped down, only to find himself in the corridor of the compliance center once again.

Again, luminous arrows upon the display panels of the walls were directing him onward to wherever the Authority next required him to attend. Through thirty minutes of corridor in the cold and solitary station, he walked. And beyond this, the immense boredom of the search station allocated for his use awaited him.

Hours seemed like days to George, as he sat at the station, studying displays of sites throughout Earth's colonized space, and yet there was no job available for him in any colony. *Are the Authority blind?* he began to think. *Can they not see that the reason there is no work is because there is no aspiration, no expansion, no courage, and no desire to reach further throughout the universe? Where civilizations stagnate but try to keep their subjects busy, believing there is nothing else in the universe, the future is only crisis and collapse. That's what this is. The Authority is desperately afraid of blaming itself and allowing the unemployed to become dissidents, so it has resorted to burdening them with guilt and meaningless tasks.*

This pattern continued for seven days. Each time George slept, he witnessed the same vision of poison gas and the flow of molten rock. Each time he woke, he trudged to the search station and complied with the instructions of his futile search for work throughout colonial space.

Then, on the afternoon of the seventh day, he was required to return for the scheduled review. It was a moment he had been waiting for, a chance to finally voice his objections to his treatment and attempt to gather more meaningful information on his situation. Was he being deceived? Why was he being treated as a criminal while in the Authority's custody, rather than the man he really was? What was the purpose of this game?

Much of the appointment took place exactly as the previous one had, except that the strain of living in a suspension cylinder and spending whole days in front of an imager was beginning to show on George's face. He had developed a tick in his left eye, and a headache had descended on him as he waited for his name to be called.

"George."

He rose, and once again sat to speak with the advisor.

"What time did you arrive at your search station yesterday?" the advisor asked.

George hesitated. "0900 hours," he responded.

"Yes, the log shows 0900 hours as your time, but there is a discrepancy. The other times in the log show an arrival at 1000 hours prior to your entry of 0900 hours. Didn't you, in fact, arrive an hour late and enter inaccurate data onto our system?"

"The system must be having difficulties. I signed in, just as I did every other day," George insisted.

"Then why does the time index not agree with your story?"

"System difficulties?"

"Oh, so our system has difficulties, does it? And how would you know?"

"I don't know."

Once again, the advisor's vacuous grey eyes were staring with false concern, directly into George's own eyes. This was beginning to grow annoying, deepening the resentment that George already felt towards this hollow parody of an official.

The advisor's hand manipulated the interactive panel as he continued to stare at George. George watched the panel, as the advisor erased the logs of his intensive actions to find work throughout the week. All those hours of searching and studying, wasted. Now, he anticipated that the advisor would lecture him, in brazen ignorance of all that he had done and every effort he had invested in the previous seven days.

"I have complied with everything you have asked me to do," George said, "what do you want?"

"But it's about more than just compliance isn't it? It's about more than just this."

George glanced at the notice on the office wall:

ANY FAILURE TO COMPLY WILL RESULT IN MEMORY ERASURE

"You'll have my memory erased, if I don't comply," he recalled from it.

"What is teamwork?" the advisor said. This time, the advisor's stare was more intense than earlier. There was neither a break, nor even a blink in the asinine contest of eye contact.

"I have had enough of your games," George said.

"That came across as condescending."

"No," George contested, "you come across as arrogant and self-indulgent. Who or what are you?"

"We can't continue this conversation," the advisor finished, "sign here."

Once again, the advisor gestured to the interactive panel on the desk. As before, George signed this with his own index finger and continued to follow further instructions. *I haven't failed to comply*, he thought, *I have only objected to this absurd treatment, so I shouldn't lose my memory.* Still, he was distressed that he had not gained any opportunity to learn more of his situation, and he departed the office quite miserably again.

Half an hour later, while checking the planning imager at his assigned sleep cylinder, he saw that he had been scheduled to sleep for only two hours before resuming his job research at the compliance center. *They are trying to kill me*, he thought, *what could they possibly accomplish from such a waste of time?*

Hastily, he stepped into his cylinder again. To him, the transition was instantaneous. From George's perspective, the cylinder closed and was already open once again, and George fell to the floor from it. Exhausted, he pulled himself to his feet. The immediate sensations were heat and thirst. Then, as he moved through the corridor, he felt disorientation. There was also hopelessness, misery and fear. In this moment, George believed that he had never felt so lost and vulnerable since his infancy. Was it a mental side-effect of such a short suspension period in the cylinder? He did not know.

He stumbled through the corridors, still seeking to comply with his instructions. *I mustn't lose my memories. I mustn't be wiped!* George thought. As he found what he thought to be the search station, the headache descended on him like a clap of thunder. As he focused, he saw that the station was only a video contact terminal. He had taken a wrong turn. Hardly able to stand, he retreated back along what he thought to be his path.

An automatic door slid open. Before he could try to pass through, intense heat and noxious fumes struck him like a wall of death, deterring him from moving any further. Through the haze, he again perceived the same hideous veins of molten rock that he had witnessed in his nightmare. *This is not real, I'm not awake,* George thought, *I must go back. I must wake from this hallucination.*

However, his attempt to withdraw back into the adjacent corridor with the terminal was met with failure. Instead, he again stood in the office, and his advisor rose in anger to find him standing, quaking on the office floor. "For failing to get to the site of the search station, you will be wiped. Your memory of these events will be purged," the advisor said.

"No!" George resisted, fleeing back through the door. Passing through the wall of fumes, he was immediately collapsing, choking on the burning black crust of the poisonous illusory landscape that had been waiting beyond the door. The advisor, in his fury, had already followed him out and witnessed the impossible landscape of noxious Hades outside his door. No sooner than he had emerged, he tripped and tumbled along a verge that led him down into the devastating heat of the molten rock. The cry of terror that followed paralyzed George with the intense fear that the same fate might soon come to him.

Crawling along the scalding alien terrain, George found the slippery base of a suspension cylinder under his palm. Its cold touch presented an invitation for him to use the machine to preserve what remained of his life. Before he could succumb to the hostile place, he had pulled himself back into the field of the cylinder, but the effects of dizziness and disorientation only grew ever more intense as he tried to rest there.

There was a violent tremor gripping the whole apparatus around him, followed by a terrible spinning sensation. After some minutes, this subsided, and George began to see the place where he had been transported in his plight. Nausea gripped him, before he stepped down onto the metal floor of a vast bay, and then fell onto his side. His lungs felt greatly burned and irritated, and every millimeter of his skin was scorched. His dehydration still pained him, and he lost consciousness as he lay on the cold metal deck stretching out before him.

It must have been hours before the darkness had subsided and he regained consciousness. After the juncture of confusion and pain had fully passed, he saw that he had already been moved to a ward in the intensive care area of a medical center. There was no difficulty in recognizing the familiar place. His dazzled eyes were still unable to pick out much detail in the intense light of the medical center, but he was able to recognize the nuances of the dear woman beside him.

"Doctor," he said, "Doctor Grady?"

"Yes, Captain?" she answered.

"What happened?"

"You were in a disc accident. You are one of three survivors in a team of five. It is just blind luck that you got out of it intact."

George felt like weeping. *I should have been the one who died, instead of our innocent guys*, he thought. Even while unconscious, he still managed to be responsible for yet more meaningless deaths, now well into the second year of exile. After a moment of mournful silence as he sat, he presented his question to the Doctor.

"I remember witnessing several days at a compliance center. How is that possible? I have never been incarcerated at one of those facilities."

"They are known to erase memories, for the protection of state secrets," Grady suggested, "our cerebral scans showed increased activity in the centers of your brain tied to long term memory. Remember, the technology to keep your brain and vital organs in emergency suspension in the event of a disc crash is basically an outgrowth of the Authority's memory-wiping technology."

"Are you saying that technology somehow restored my memory? How long was I out there?"

"You were out there for around four minutes. Any longer would have been lethal. The Bridge had found the disc, patched it, and salvaged it almost as soon as the accident occurred."

"It seemed like a week, from my perspective."

"Our sense of time is tied to the memory centers of our brains. If you recovered a week of your lost memories, it should be no surprise that you think you were out there for a week, and that you think you were at the compliance center during that time."

"I had no knowledge of my time at a compliance center. If they escaped with that unconscionable trickery, what else has the Authority escaped with on Earth?"

"One of the greatest things about our exile, if nothing else," Grady concluded, "is our freedom to reflect on what the Authority would have done to us if we were still in their hands."

Nodding thoughtfully, George swallowed. He looked away in shame, as the Doctor continued to observe. *To have parts of my life censored in my own head!* he thought. *And for that to contain episodes of torture, threats, brain manipulation and abuse perpetrated by a regime desperate to hide its own crisis! Up until now, I had never thought our exile on this lost ship was fortunate.*

But if our government has degenerated as much as I have seen, then ours is not the ship of fools at all. Perhaps there could be no gladder fate than to be onboard my ship, even as she resumes her course to nowhere.

BONUS STORY: "SO FAR AWAY" (flash fiction)

Originally published on 9 July 2014 in *FlashFiction Magazine*

As he seated himself at the glossy black coffee table, reflecting the infinite depths of the looming constellations through the large window of the Officer's Lounge, Captain Sannox felt wistful. Beyond the hardened pane of transparent alloy waited everything, and yet nothing. As he gazed there, space itself seemed to stare back ominously.

In truth, there was no course. Nearly a thousand people under his command were being taken further and further from their home with every passing day, and each day the chances of them ever returning to Earth became more and more astronomical. Their destination: nowhere.

Science Observer Wade interceded, "George, what's on your mind?"

"Our mission," Sannox said, "what are we searching for out here?"

Wade gave a look of concentration, for a moment. "We fled the Solar Authority, due to its xenophobia and oppression," he reminded the Captain. "Perhaps we'll never return. But our lives mean something, as long as we can maintain a living community aboard *Traction*."

"I've led them astray, all of them," Sannox said.

"Well, who's to say we won't eventually return?" Wade suggested.

"Right now, we're safe. If our sole objective was to escape, we have accomplished it. So, why not cut power to the engines and live out the rest of our lives on *Traction*?" Sannox suggested.

Wade looked at Sannox in disbelief, and the Captain continued. "Is it time for us to turn back? Has our search for safety by fleeing the Authority's space been a waste of time? Do we not, eventually, need to return home to face justice?" Sannox asked.

"We are not here as some kind of selfish exercise to prolong our lives," Wade said, "we are here to explore. Our civilization has reached a point of crisis. You have said that, yourself. The only way that we can resolve this crisis is by discovering new worlds, new species, new technologies, new futures, and new kinds of existence. If the crew didn't understand this, they would have mutinied in turn against you. You command this ship, because this crew respects its Captain. There is nothing official in it, at this point. People believe in this journey."

"How could you possibly know that?"

"Because they signed a petition," Wade said. "The crew understands why we are out here, and they have committed to this journey. Human existence is a course to nowhere, George. What we are doing is glorious."

"A petition questioning the orders of the Captain is not acceptable onboard a Solar Navy starship."

"This isn't just a ship. It's our home. Where else could we have an honest conversation about our future?"

Sannox knew what it meant, but he was determined not to show any sign of satisfaction. "Earth," he said, as his eyes returned to the big observation window. "It's so distant now, it's irrelevant. So far away, a thing might as well not exist."

We may be the only humans for nearly a thousand light-years. And what does that make me? Sannox thought. *I feel like the leader of a whole species, isolated in the universe.*

BONUS STORY: "NAVIGATING ETERNITY" (short fiction)

Only available in Ship of Fools

Claps of solid matter against the hull sent devastating vibrations along every deck of the starship *Traction*. Instantly, her Computer recognized the futility of continuing, and she drew to a sudden halt among the smattering of obstructing particles that had collided with her.

Some millions of kilometers behind the ship's position, the tower of sensor devices nicknamed the "Nest" had alerted the vessel quickly enough to avert any serious penetration of the hull. However, the Captain was still outraged. He rose from his chair, gesticulating in anger. "Who navigated this?" he raged in the direction of his nearest subordinates sitting at the immensely complex right wing navigation board.

"Whoever or whatever made the error, they're in a black zone. We can't see the problem," Tech Ferguson said mysteriously, leaning over the board to study his readings.

"What the heck is that supposed to mean, Ferguson?" Sannox demanded, "we could have been destroyed. Do you have any idea of the speeds of the objects hitting us? Send repair teams to all the affected sections. I want a full report, immediately."

"No damage sustained to any regeneration nodes. Hull armor was not penetrated," Ferguson reported.

"Where is the unresponsive system?" Sannox asked, as Engineer John Harmer stepped onto the deck from a nearby personnel lift and awaited orders from his Captain.

"The–" Ferguson hesitated.

"Yes, Mr. Ferguson?" Sannox prompted, "where is it?"

"–the Forbidden Capsule, Nexus Tower, Nest Section."

"Harmer?" Sannox said, turning to his Engineer for more information.

"The Forbidden Capsule," Harmer began cautiously, "the Capsule is the only part of the ship that we are not authorized to enter. Only admirals and Solar Fleet flag officers are authorized to look inside."

"Surely you must mean that there is sensitive information stored there," Sannox said, "is it a terminal of sorts?"

Harmer's eye contact drifted away from his Captain to meet the floor. This seldom happened, and Sannox thought it was as if the cold hand of the earthbound Authority had stretched out across thousands of light-years to land on his shoulder.

"Harmer? What is it?" Sannox prompted.

"I don't know what is in the Capsule."

"I would like to hear your guess," Sannox suggested.

"I–" the Engineer stalled.

The Captain was astonished. *John has never been stumped like this before. What in a thousand worlds is wrong with the man?* he thought. "Do you mean to say that you were never mentored on the purpose of that part of the ship?"

"You know we have dark zones," Harmer said, "self-sustaining scientific instruments so complex that no individual on this ship has any training to handle them."

"You are saying it is an instrument?" Sannox asked.

"No," Harmer attempted to reply.

"But surely you mean it, *whatever it is*, is techno-scientific in nature, and you are the most highly qualified man we have to deal with it?"

Harmer straightened his black fatigue shirt. "Of course," he said.

"We're going take a look inside the Capsule, and see just what the Authority doesn't want us to see," the Captain declared. At this moment, the Bridge fell silent. With this conclusion, the Engineer and the Captain both stepped onto the cold and heavy cargo lift preferred by Sannox as his means of reaching through the spine of the immense vessel.

While they rode in the lift, Sannox and Harmer spoke again. "You seem a little apprehensive about this," Sannox said. "Remember, we have already turned against the Authority. Whatever rules they invented for us to follow, they are now irrelevant.

"What kind of rule is that, anyway? Not permitting an Engineer to see the systems he is charged with maintaining?"

"Perhaps it is something so sensitive that our presence would contaminate it. That's what is making me apprehensive about all this," Harmer said.

"You said the Capsule is restricted to flag officers, not engineering experts," the Captain reminded, "I get a strong sense that this restriction is political or ethical, rather than being based on an engineering issue. If that does turn out to be the case, your services will no doubt be required. " Sannox received no reply from Harmer. *Contaminate?* the Captain thought, *is that really possible? Could there be a system sensitive to our presence, and with inadequate shielding? What would be the practicality in that kind of engineering?*

The ride in the cargo lift ended, revealing a small metallic space when the doors of the lift had withdrawn. Sannox had never visited such a small space in the immense vessel, nor had he ever been given any training on this obscure part of the Nest. *I always knew there were areas that I hadn't been trained in, and were left to the engineers,* he thought, *but I never imagined walking into an obscure part of the ship in search of a vital system.*

At the far side of the small floor of metal, there stood a large barrier constructed from a darker alloy, and the foot of this barrier was demarcated by a double red line of paint. Sannox had only seen such a mark before in a vital Fleet facility. It indicated a zone that could not be crossed without direct authorization from the highest officials of the Solar Authority. As he approached these lines, even the Captain was beginning to detect a tremulous sense of dread in his own footsteps.

As he stood before the dark barrier, he turned to see that Harmer had not stepped forward. Inscribed in small white letters on the barrier were the words:

WARNING: For the Consultation of the Earth Solar Treaty Organization Secretary General, Navy Admirals and Flag Officers Only

Beneath this inscription, there was a small panel. Sannox's own sense of uncertainty was growing ever stronger in the face of the self-important inscription and panel left by vain men and authorities resting thousands of light-years behind him. He saw no option other than to continue, so he gestured to his Engineer to attend the panel.

Stepping back, the Captain watched as Harmer came forward. He pulled the panel, and it collapsed heavily to the deck plate. A red lever had been exposed, with a flickering light at the side. Harmer pulled the lever down, and the dark barrier began to rise.

Behind the barrier, a transparent vat stood like an aquarium. Within it, some entity stirred in the darkness. It was impossible to see it clearly, but something about the thing's movements gave rise to a brewing and irrepressible sense of dread in Sannox's heart.

For nearly a minute, Sannox and Harmer both stood in confusion at the purpose of such an apparatus. A light descended, and there was a burst of green fluid within the vat. From within that gas, the stirring figure emerged. Naked, and with bloodless white skin, the thing was scarcely even humanoid. The head was grotesquely large at the back, belying the cybernetic implants at the base of the pipes and cables protruding from behind it. Above the creature, an array of hypodermic syringes extended from a ring attached to a robotic arm.

The creature was blind, staring with the pales of its eyes into eternity.

"Bastards," Sannox mouthed. He was afraid to speak aloud, out of concern that it might somehow disturb the sensitive creature enslaved in the vat.

"It's an artificial host, a synthetic life-form, used as a navigational aid among the unexpected hazards of interstellar space. Hazards that no machine can anticipate," Harmer said, in a shaking voice. "This form of slavery was officially banned by the Authority. I had no idea that we were relying on it to coordinate our Stiletto Class ships, the entire time. It is resting. George, what are our orders?"

Captain Sannox was silent, anger propelling every muscle of his body to break the glass and save the tortured being behind it. Finally, he turned away, with a profound sense of hopelessness and dismay at this infinite cruelty of his own species. Not willing to speak, he gestured for his Engineer to close the barrier and restore the Navigator to his solitude.

This creature is essential to the ship, Sannox concluded in his thoughts. *I cannot reveal it to the crew. Now, I understand the cruel reality of why this slave must be concealed from my subordinates. I abhor whoever chose to introduce these entities aboard our ships, enslaving, abusing and perverting living brains for use as navigational aids. Without these creatures, our ships could not navigate safely through the infinite perilous objects of space. I hate this necessity. However, under the pressure of command, I am compelled to perpetuate this abhorrent crime, rather than permit the destruction of my entire ship and crew.*